This picture book helps children learn about mathematical concepts through a colorful and entertaining story.

Math concepts explored may include:
- Understanding math concepts
- Classifying and placing in order
- Placing in order, complex classification, organizing data, and predicting future outcomes

About the Author
Ae-hae Yoon has a master's degree in children's literature from Sungkyunkwan University in Seoul, South Korea. She teaches children's literature to teachers in training. Ae-hae has written many children's books.

About the Illustrator
Hae-won Yang graduated with a degree in visual design from Seoul Women's University. An active member of the South Korean Publishing Illustration Association, Hae-won has illustrated many children's books.

Tan Tan Math Story ***Who Eats First?***

Original Korean edition © Yeowon Media Co., Ltd

This U.S edition published in 2015 by TANTAN PUBLISHING INC, 4005 W Olympic Blvd, Los Angeles, CA 90019-3258

U.S and Canada Edition © TANTAN PUBLISHING INC in 2015

ISBN: 978-1-939248-00-8

Printed in South Korea at Choil Munhwa Printing Co., 12 Seongsuiro 20 gil, Seongdong-gu, Seoul.

Who Eats First?

Written by Ae-hae Yoon **Illustrated by Hae-won Yang**

✿TanTan Publishing

The rain forest animals were hungry.
They followed a sweet scent. . . .
And there was a BIG round peach!
Surely, it was a *delicious* peach.
But who would eat the first bite?

The gangly giraffe, the greedy alligator, and the roly-poly rhino—each wanted to taste that *delicious* peach! The tricky monkey, the bouncy rabbit, and the wiggly caterpillar each wanted to eat first, too.

Giraffe thought for a minute, then stretched his neck longer. "Ahem," he said, "it's best if **the tallest animal** eats first. I wonder who is tallest. We'll have to measure."

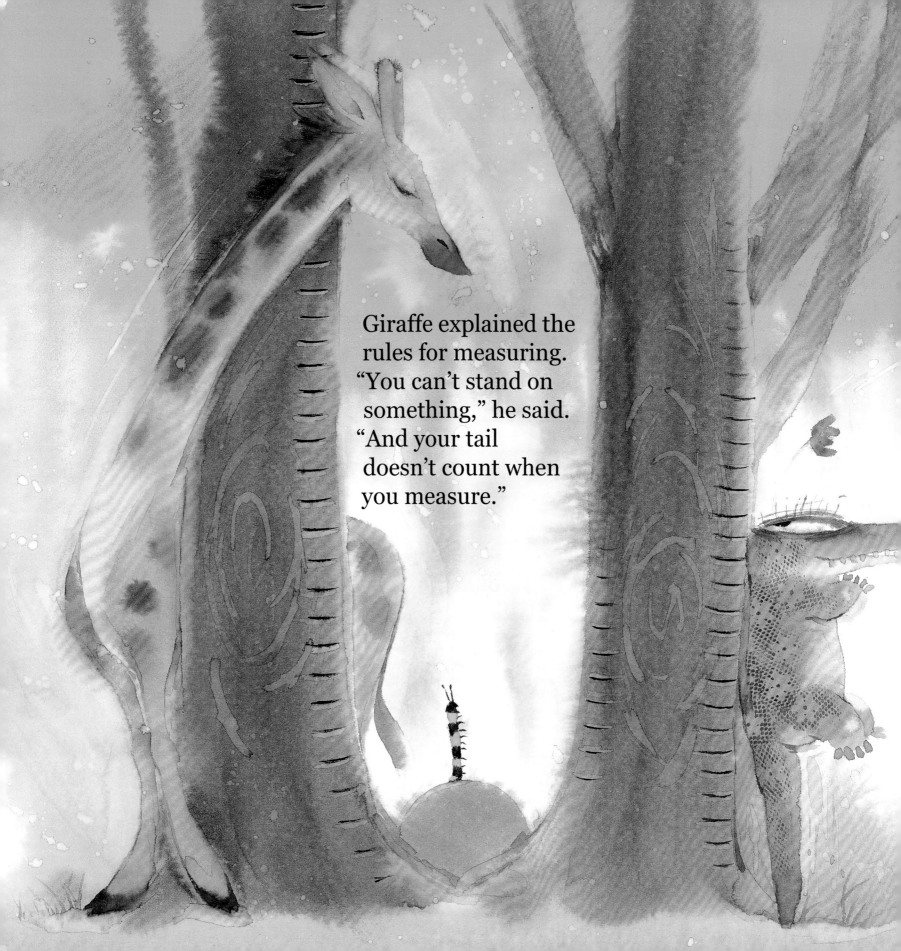

Giraffe explained the
rules for measuring.
"You can't stand on
something," he said.
"And your tail
doesn't count when
you measure."

Rabbit had a rule, too. "You can't rise up on your tiptoes, either," she said.

"It's all clear now," said Giraffe. "I will eat first because *I'm* **the tallest animal**!" Giraffe stretched his neck even longer. But just as he was about to eat the BIG round peach . . .

Rhino had an idea. "No!" he said. "For a peach this big, **the heaviest animal** should eat first." He pounded the ground with his hoof to show he was serious. "Here's how we'll measure each animal's weight."

"Let's make a seesaw and use it to measure everyone's weight. An animal sits on one end of the seesaw. Then we'll pile rocks on the other end. When the seesaw is evenly balanced, we'll count the rocks piled up for each animal. The animal balanced by the most rocks is the heaviest!"

The animals got busy measuring
one another's weight. Who
would be the heaviest?

"See? *I'm the heaviest*!" Rhino shouted. "I get to eat first!" But as rhino thundered toward the BIG round peach . . .

Gator opened his huge slurpy mouth.
"No!" he said. "For a peach this big, it makes
sense for **the animal with the biggest mouth**
to eat first."

The contest was on! Whose mouth was the biggest?

"My mouth is **the biggest by far**!" roared Rhino

"Mine is bigger!" snapped Gator.

"There's no doubt about it," said Gator. "Because my mouth is **the biggest**, "*I* will eat first." Gator opened his mouth wide. But just as he was about to bite into the BIG round peach . . .

Rabbit bounced by with her ears perked up. "No way!" she said. **"The animal with the longest ears will eat first!"**

Rabbit perched on Giraffe's back.
"Line up to see who has the
longest ears," she said. "I knew
it—mine are **the longest**!"

"Nonsense!" shouted Monkey,
who was hanging upside down.
"Whoever has the longest tail
should be the first to eat!"

"When it comes to tails, *I'm* first,"
Monkey said, waving his long tail.
"But who is second?"

Gator looked back at his own tail. "Hmmm, I don't know where my tail begins," he said.

The caterpillar had been quietly watching the other animals. She was so tiny, the others had barely noticed her.

"Why should **the biggest animal** eat first?" Caterpillar asked. "Or **the heaviest animal** or **the one with the biggest mouth**—or even **the one with the longest ears**?"

"If we measure **from the shortest** to the tallest animal, I'm first."

"Or **from the lightest** to the heaviest, I'm first again!"

"Measuring **from the shortest ears** to the longest . . .
Well, I have no ears, which makes me number one!"

"And going **from the smallest mouth** to the biggest, I'm still first."

Caterpillar had more to say.
"And if we measure **from the shortest tail**
to the longest, I'm f-i-r-s-t! " she said.
"Here's the deal. If we start from the smallest
in everything, I'm first, first, and *always*
first! That means *I'm* the animal who eats
first. And I *do* love sweet, juicy peaches!"

Caterpillar dove into the BIG round peach.

Comparing and Placing in Order

Placing in order, along with classifying, is an essential process for organizing data. To place objects in order, one must first compare them. When one compares objects based on a criterion, a sequence results, and that sequence has a clear direction and pattern. For example, when one arranges three cars of different sizes in order, the cars can be arranged as: the biggest car, the medium-sized car, and the smallest car. The direction of this order is from big to small, and the pattern reflects the order of size. The direction of the order can be changed. The cars could be arranged from smallest to biggest.

Help students or children organize and arrange objects based on various characteristics. Household objects such as shoes, books, spoons, and socks work well for this activity. Leaves, twigs, stones, and other things collected outdoors also work well. Extend the activity by having students reorder the objects by changing the criterion, which will help them grasp comparing, classifying, and reordering.

All in Order, One by One

| **Activity Goal** | To place objects in order by length (size)
| **Materials** | Various household objects* (kitchen items, socks, toys), cardboard, scissors, pencil or marker, ruler
| **Players** | 3–6

1 This game is an indoor activity. Make cardboard playing cards in numerical order, in sync with the number of players. For example, if there are 4 players, prepare 4 cards numbered: ①, ②, ③, ④. One number appears on only one side of each card.

2 Place the cards with the numbered sides facedown and rearrange them randomly. Each person picks a card and keeps it in his/her pocket. It's OK to look at the number on your card.

3 Within the space of the game area, each player selects one object. Limit the time for selecting the items to 5 minutes.

4 Arrange the objects in order. The shortest (or the smallest) object will be placed first. The second-shortest object will be placed to the right of the first object. Continue with sorting and ordering until all objects are placed in order.

5 Have all players remove the cards from their pockets and arrange them in numerical order matching the placed objects. If a player has the numerical card that matches his/her object in the sequence, that player is a winner. There can be more than one winner in this game. All players congratulate and applaud the winners!

* The objects must be easy to carry—not too heavy or too big.

Why Was the Caterpillar the First to Eat?

The rain forest animals ordered themselves in many different ways in an effort to decide who should eat the peach first. Ultimately, the caterpillar argued her case most persuasively—and so she was the first animal to eat the peach.

The giraffe was the tallest. But if measuring **from shortest to tallest**, the caterpillar was first.

The rhino was the heaviest. But measuring **from lightest to heaviest**, the caterpillar was first again.

The alligator had the biggest mouth. But measuring **from the smallest mouth to the biggest**, the caterpillar was once again first.

The rabbit had the longest ears. But measuring **from the shortest ears to the longest**—sure enough, the caterpillar was first, because it has no ears.

Placing Toys in Order

The toys are in a jumble—it's time to organize them! Get started by placing them against the wall in order. But in what order?

Ordered by height, the princess doll is first.

Ordered by weight, the teddy bear is first.

Ordered by nose length, the wooden puppet with the long nose is first.

Ordered by **number of legs**, the ant is first, because he has six legs!